Junkyard Dan

Stuffed Animal

NOX PRESS
books for that extra kick to give you more power
www.NoxPress.com

Also by Elise Leonard:

The **JUNKYARD DAN** series: (***Nox Press***)

1. Start of a New Dan
2. Dried Blood
3. Stolen?
4. Gun in the Back
5. Plans
6. Money for Nothing
7. Stuffed Animal
8. Poison, Anyone?
9. A Picture Tells a Thousand Dollars
10. Wrapped Up
11. Finished
12. Bloody Knife
13. Taking Names and Kicking Assets
14. Mercy

THE SMITH BROTHERS (a series): (***Nox Press***)

1. All for One
2. When in Rome
3. Get a Clue
4. The Hard Way
5. Master Plan

A LEEG OF HIS OWN (a series): (***Nox Press***)

1. Croaking Bullfrogs, Hidden Robbers
2. 20,000 LEEGS Under the C
3. Failure to Lunch
4. Hamlette

The **AL'S WORLD** series: (***Simon & Schuster***)

Book 1: Monday Morning Blitz
Book 2: Killer Lunch Lady
Book 3: Scared Stiff
Book 4: Monkey Business

The **LEADER** series: (***Nox Press***)

★ Honor
★ Courage
★ Respect
★ Service
★ Integrity
★ Commitment
★ Loyalty
★ Duty

PETE'S PLACE (a series): (***Nox Press***)

1. On Ice
2. Coffee to Go

Junkyard Dan

Stuffed Animal

Elise Leonard

NOX PRESS
books for that extra kick to give you more power
www.NoxPress.com

Leonard, Elise
Junkyard Dan series / Stuffed Animal
ISBN 978-0-9815694-6-8

Copyright © 2008 by Elise Leonard.
All rights reserved, including the right of reproduction in whole or in part in any form. Published by Nox Press.
www.NoxPress.com

First Nox Press printing: October 2008
Second Nox Press printing: October 2009
Third Nox Press printing: September 2010

books for that extra kick to give you more power

To my readers:

Wow, guys,
I can't thank you enough
for your cool letters and emails!
Thanks for letting me share your joyful pride
on your road to a better life through literacy.

You're working hard,
you're doing it,
you're accomplishing your goals,
and I'm honored that you read my books.

You guys are my heroes.

Keep up the great work!

Thanks to Connie Buggica for taking the cover art photo. And many thanks to her parents for allowing us to use a picture of their beautiful home
and their Cadillac.

~Elise

Chapter 1

I was just getting to know Rosa.

And now it was time for her to go.

She wasn't here long. And her reason for being here? Not good. Her father had passed away.

But she had been here. In Peaceville. And I was glad to have met her.

So glad, I was sorry to see her go.

Really sorry.

Sorry... and sad.

"You have everything?" I asked her.

She grimaced and nodded. "Yes."

I nodded.

We stood there quietly.

The bus station was crowded. People all over

the place.

There wasn't much privacy.

But we really didn't need it.

We didn't know each other that well.

But I wanted to see her off.

So did her old friends. My new friends. Bubba, Mel and Henry, Miles and Judge Simpkins.

"I'm sorry about your dad," I said. "But I'm glad I got to meet you."

I felt awkward. Clumsy.

Like a little kid again. Not a grown man.

"I was glad to meet you too, Dan," she said.

She sounded a little breathless. Like she was having trouble saying goodbye as well.

"*I need everyone on the bus now, please*," the bus driver called out.

The loudspeakers crackled.

"Last call for bus number 1163. Last call for bus number 1163. If you have a ticket for bus 1163? Please board the bus now."

I looked at Rosa.

She was looking at me.

Stuffed Animal

Her usual dark skin looked a little pale.

Her big brown eyes were floating in tears.

Her cute nose was pink.

She hugged us all, and kissed our cheeks. Then she got on the bus.

I watched the bus drive away.

I watched the bus turn the corner.

I stood there for fifteen minutes.

For some reason? I didn't want to leave.

Judge Simpkins moved next to me.

"You okay, son?" he asked gently.

I nodded.

I didn't feel like talking. Not about that.

So I'd just nodded.

I turned to my friends. "If you don't mind? I think I'll just go home," I said.

"Yeah," Bubba said. "Me too."

"Mind if I catch a ride with you?" Miles asked me.

"Sure," I told him.

"I think I'll go fishing," Judge Simpkins muttered.

Chapter 2

When I got home? The phone was ringing.

My heart quickened.

Maybe it was Rosa. But probably not.

She was still on the bus. Going home.

I unlocked the door as fast as I could.

I grabbed the phone.

Maybe it was a customer. That would be good.

Something to get my mind off of Rosa.

I didn't know how long it was ringing. But I didn't want them to hang up.

I ran to the phone. The one in my office.

"Hello?" I shouted into the phone.

"Hello?" a young woman said.

Again, my heart quickened.

Stuffed Animal

For a second? I thought it might be Rosa.

But it wasn't her.

Rosa had an accent. Her voice had a lilt to it.

It was almost musical.

This woman didn't have an accent.

Well, maybe a little accent. A southern accent.

Rosa's was different.

Rosa spoke Spanish fluently. It was her first language as a child. So her accent was shaped by that.

Rosa had a beautiful accent.

"Is this Dan?" the caller asked sharply.

For a second? I forgot about the woman on the phone.

I'd been thinking about Rosa. Again.

"Yes," I said. "This is Dan."

"I have your name. As a last resort."

"A last resort?" I asked.

"Before an animal gets put down," she said.

Her comment shocked me a little.

"Excuse me?" I said.

"I'm calling from the animal shelter."

Oh. Now I got it.

She must mean the other Dan. Old Dan. The *former* Junkyard Dan.

"You must be calling for Dan," I said.

"I thought *you* were Dan," she said.

"Well, I am," I said slowly.

"I'm confused," she said dryly.

"It's a long story," I said.

"Look. I have a dog. He'll be put down this afternoon if I can't find someone. I've been trying to call you all morning," she rushed. "I have no one else."

"Put down as in… killed?" I asked.

"Yes."

"Why are they going to kill him?" I asked.

"He's a tough case," she said. "Beaten. Badly. He must have run away."

I pictured the dog.

"When we got him? He was filthy. Almost starving to death," she said briskly.

I thought of that poor dog. Thought of his life.

Life as he'd known it.

Stuffed Animal

He hadn't *asked* to be put in that situation.

What living thing would?!

Nothing deserved to be beaten and starved.

Not a person. Not an animal. Not a living thing.

"How can I help?" I asked.

She waited before she spoke.

As if she were trying to think of a good way to say what she had to say.

"He's not good with people," she said. "Doesn't trust them."

I snorted a laugh. But felt no humor.

"Can you blame him?" I asked her.

"No. But I can't put him with a family. It's too risky," she said.

I nodded.

I knew she couldn't see me.

"He trusts other dogs, though," she said. "He seems to trust *all* animals. Cats, too."

I thought of my dogs and cats. All playing together.

All living together. Peacefully.

"I'll come get him," I said. "Where are you?"

Chapter 3

I heard a rush of breath come out of her.

Like she'd been holding her breath.

"I'm so glad," she said with emotion. "Relieved."

I smiled.

"The Dan on your list is the old Dan," I told her.

"The old Dan?" she asked.

"The former owner," I explained. "He passed away."

"Oh," she said. "This may change things."

She sounded nervous.

"Do you feel the same way?" she asked me. "About animals?"

Stuffed Animal

That made me chuckle.

"Well, if you would have asked me a while ago? I don't know how I'd have answered you."

"But now?" she asked slowly.

I laughed again.

"Now that I *have* so many?" I told her. "It seems that I do."

Again, I heard the breath whoosh out of her.

"I'm so glad," she said.

I was glad too.

"How many animals *do* you have?" she asked.

That made me crack up. "A bunch."

She laughed too.

"Good," she said.

"So when can I pick him up?" I asked.

She stayed quiet for a minute.

"Will it be okay if I brought him to you?" she asked.

I wondered why she'd ask that.

"Sure," I said.

"I just want to make sure he's okay with the placement," she said.

Oh. I got it.

They wanted to check *me* out. Since they didn't know me.

"That's fine. You'll see that I take good care of everyone here," I said proudly.

And I did!

A good man takes care of those around him.

I'd like to think I'm a good man.

"Oh," she said. "I'm not worried about *you*."

"You're not?" I asked.

"No."

"Oh. Good," I said.

I still wondered why she wanted to come here.

It would be easier for her if I went there.

"We want…" she started to say.

Then she started again.

"*I* want… to make sure he's happy there," she said.

"Oh," I said. "Okay."

I shrugged my shoulders.

"This is the last stop for him," she said.

I didn't get what she meant.

Stuffed Animal

"The last stop?" I asked.

She whispered her reply. "If this doesn't work out? We'll be forced to put him down."

That shocked me.

"I'm his last hope?" I asked softly.

"Yes."

I didn't know what to say.

"That's why it's important that this work out," she said.

I needed to ask.

"Is he that bad?"

"He's been horribly abused," she said quietly. "He doesn't seem to like people."

My heart went out to this animal.

"He will learn to trust here," was all I said.

Chapter 4

As I waited for the new dog, Miles came over.

"So what's up?" Miles asked me.

"I'm waiting for a lady about a dog," I said.

"Don't you mean you're waiting for a man about a horse?" he asked me.

"No," I said.

Miles waited for the punch line.

"I really *am* waiting," I told him.

"For a lady?" he asked.

"Yes," I said. "With a dog."

He grinned. "Oh. I thought it was a joke."

I shook my head.

"No," I said. "No joke."

"Want to tell me about it?" he asked.

Stuffed Animal

"He's been abused. He's about to be put down. I am his last hope," I said. "Here. At the junkyard."

Miles nodded. He was serious now.

"I'm glad you're taking him," Miles said. "Dan would have."

It was my turn to nod.

"I know. He was a good man," I said.

"Speaking of good men..." Miles said. He whipped out that old stuffed animal again. "What are we going to do about this?"

He wiggled the old bear.

The toy's head bobbled side to side.

It looked well worn. Well loved.

Like the stuffing had be squeezed down. From too many hugs.

Too many nights sharing a crib or bed with a child.

Too many hours of being crushed between small, clammy hands.

"Do you really think it belonged to that boy?" I asked Miles. "The one who was kidnapped?"

"I don't know," he answered. "But it can't hurt to find out."

"No," I said. "I guess not."

Miles shrugged. "Better to be safe…"

I nodded. "…than sorry."

Miles looked at the bear. "Yes."

Just then there was a knock at the door.

I heard a dog bark at the sound.

The knock had set him off.

His bark was loud. Vicious.

It sounded savage. Untamed.

I wondered what I'd gotten myself into.

"Sounds like he's got some issues," Miles said softly.

Miles was talking about the dog.

And he *did* sound like he had issues.

Big issues.

Anger issues.

Again, I wondered what I'd gotten myself into.

I walked to the door.

Miles was right behind me.

I stretched to open the screen door.

Stuffed Animal

The dog growled loudly.

He showed his teeth.

"Please," the woman said slowly. "Move slowly. Speak gently."

The dog was pulling at the leash. Trying to get at me.

At least I thought he was.

He seemed to be standing his ground.

Showing who was boss.

Trying to, at least.

This was one ill-treated dog.

It was obvious that he'd been beaten.

I moved to open the screen door.

He was hand shy.

He flinched for just a second.

But that flinch told me a lot.

Just after he cowered, he showed his teeth again.

He was angry. *Very* angry.

Then he started barking wildly.

My dogs came running. They wanted to see what all the fuss was about.

Elise Leonard

They crowded around him.

At first he kept his teeth showing.

But quickly, he calmed.

The dogs did what dogs do.

You know. They, ah, sniffed each others' butts.

That took a while.

(There were a lot of butts *to* sniff.)

I noticed that he was no longer growling. Or showing his teeth.

He seemed to like the other dogs.

Some cats started coming over too.

They looked at him with boredom.

He looked back at them.

He didn't growl at them. He didn't chase them.

He accepted them.

They accepted him.

There was no challenge. By anyone.

He'd been accepted. Approved.

And he'd accepted them.

If only people could be the same way.

Without the butt sniffing, of course.

Chapter 5

"Does he have a name?" I asked the woman.

"No," she said. "I was afraid to name him. Just in case."

"So what should I name him?" I asked aloud.

She shrugged.

So did Miles.

I looked at the poor animal.

I could see scars on his exposed skin. He had open, festering sores.

He walked with a limp.

I wondered if his limp was from a beating.

I wondered if it would go away.

"I think I'll call him Lucky," I announced.

"*Lucky*?!" the woman and Miles said at the

same time.

"He doesn't seem all that lucky to me!" Miles said.

The woman agreed.

"He is from now on," I said with a smile.

The woman was beaming.

"Yes," she said. "From this day forward, he *is* lucky."

I looked at Miles. "What do you think?"

Miles looked at the dog.

The dog was surrounded by animals.

Just then? I was shocked by what I saw.

"Did you see that?" I said.

"Yes," the woman whispered.

"I can't believe my eyes," Miles said.

I couldn't believe my eyes either!

The dog started wagging his tail.

That's right. Wagging his tail.

"Since we got him? He's never done that," the woman said.

"Never?" Miles asked her.

She shook her head.

Stuffed Animal

"Never."

Miles looked back at the dog.

He started to chuckle. His laughter bubbled up from deep within his chest.

It was a low rumbling sound.

"Well look at that," Miles said.

"Yes," the woman said. "Look at that."

It was a sight to behold.

"So?" I asked Miles. "What do you think of the name?"

"Lucky it is," Miles said.

Chapter 6

The woman turned to leave.

"I think he'll be very happy here," she said with joy.

"I hope so," I said.

She smiled.

"I think things will work out just fine," Miles said.

The woman looked at me. "Well, if not? Just call me. I'll come get him."

Her face twitched when she said that.

I knew what she was thinking.

If she came back here? It was curtains for Lucky.

It would be the end of his unlucky life. His

Stuffed Animal

short unlucky life.

"Don't worry," I said. "I won't call."

She tried to smile.

"If you need to…" she said.

I shook my head.

I smiled softly.

"There will be no reason to call," I said.

She looked back at the dog.

He looked like he would be okay.

"Please," I told her. "Don't worry."

Miles looked at her.

In his deep voice he said, "I know. With children and animals, it's hard not to worry."

That got me thinking of that teddy bear.

As soon as she left, I turned to Miles.

"Let's at least try to find out. You know, if the bear belonged to that boy."

Miles smiled.

"You're a good man, Dan Corbett."

I waved off his words.

"Do you remember what I said to you when we first met?" Miles asked me.

I didn't know what he was asking about.

He'd said a lot of things.

"I said that you'd missed something. Because you hadn't met Dan," Miles said.

Oh. Yes. I remembered that.

"But you want to know what?" Miles asked me.

"What?" I asked.

"Dan had missed a lot, too. By not meeting you," Miles said.

That made me smile.

"Dan would have liked you," Miles said.

His deep voice was so soothing. It gave comfort.

"You would have liked each other," he added. "Greatly."

I took that as a compliment.

"Thank you, Miles. That means a lot to me."

Miles just smiled.

"So let's go online. Let's see if we can track down the pictures you saw of the bear," I said.

Miles nodded.

"If it's not the same bear? It's no use doing all

Stuffed Animal

that work," he said.

So we went over to my computer.

I pulled up a chair for him.

Then we Googled the kidnapping.

And like Miles said, they showed pictures of the teddy bear.

I looked at the photos. Then I looked at the bear.

"It sure does look just like it," I noted.

"Exactly like it," Miles agreed.

"Except for the arm being sewn back on," I said.

"Yes," Miles said. "I noticed that too."

"Do you think it could be another bear?" I asked.

Miles pointed to the screen.

"Look," he said. "The fur is worn in the same exact spot."

I looked back and forth.

First at the picture. Then at the teddy bear.

"That *does* make it seem similar," I said.

"The bow is exactly the same," Miles said.

"Yes," I agreed. "There's that, too."

We kept looking back and forth.

"Turn it over," Miles said.

I flipped the teddy bear. He was now back side up. Or should I say… backside up.

That didn't help much.

The picture only showed the bear's front side.

"Go back to the front," Miles said.

I flipped it back to the front.

When I flipped it around? The bear's eye wobbled.

It hung down a bit.

Like the thread that held it on was loose.

I looked at the picture.

Zoomed in on it.

"Look, Miles," I said.

I pointed to the picture.

Then I pointed to the bear.

"Even the eye is lopsided."

We looked at each other.

"That's the same bear!" we said together.

Chapter 7

"What should we do?" I asked Miles.

He was looking at the bear.

"I think we should call the parents," he said.

"Are you sure?" I asked.

Miles thought about that. "I'd want to know. If I were them."

He had a point.

I wasn't a parent. But if I had a child? I think I'd want to know.

"Do you know if they ever found the boy?" I asked.

I was still living in New York when the boy was kidnapped. It had happened about two years earlier. But the media had splashed the story across the entire country.

Miles shook his head.

"I don't know. I don't remember that part."

I didn't recall that part either. I remembered the kidnapping. But I couldn't recall the results.

"What if the boy was killed?" I said aloud.

Miles looked at me.

"Do you think the parents would want the bear? You know. If the boy was killed?" I asked him.

Miles thought about that.

"I don't know. I know *I* would," he said.

Once again I wondered about Miles.

I wondered if he had kids.

I wondered if he was married.

I wondered if he'd ever been married.

Or if he'd ever had kids.

There was so much I didn't know about Miles.

"What about you?" he asked me.

"I've never had kids," I said.

"No," he said. "I mean, would you want to know? About the bear?"

I didn't know.

Stuffed Animal

I had no clue.

I'd never had kids. So I don't know how I'd feel.

I thought about Lucky.

I know I only had him for less than an hour.

But if I could find out what had happened to him? Find out why he was the way he was?

I'd want to know.

No matter how badly it hurt to hear.

I mean, if he could *live* it? I could hear about it.

The same thing with the boy, I guess.

If he had to live through something bad? His parents might want to find out all they could about it.

But I wasn't sure.

I'd never been in that position.

Then it hit me.

"Let's ask Judge Simpkins."

"Didn't he say he was going fishing?" Miles asked.

"I know just where to find him," I told Miles.

"Okay," Miles said.

He started to get up to leave.

"Hey," I said to him. "Want to come with me?"

Miles squinted.

"Where?" he asked.

"In the canoe. Down the river. To find the judge."

Miles smiled slowly.

"I haven't been in a canoe in ages."

"It's actually very nice," I told him.

"I would imagine so," Miles said.

"So? What do you think?"

"Okay," he said slowly. "I'm in. Let's go."

He looked at me and smiled.

"How bad can it be?" he asked.

"You'll like it," I told him.

Chapter 8

We found the judge just where I thought he'd be.

"Hi Dan," the judge called.

Miles was in back. He steered the canoe right next to the judge.

He was better at guiding the canoe than I was.

"You've done this before. Haven't you," I said to Miles.

"Miles is an old pro," Judge Simpkins told me.

I turned to look over my shoulder.

Miles was a surprise a minute.

With each new day? I learned that he had another talent.

"Is there anything you *can't* do?" I asked

Miles.

Miles thought about that.

Finally he spoke.

"I can't give birth," he said.

"Thank goodness for that," Judge Simpkins said.

I turned to the judge. I hitched my thumb over my shoulder.

"Yeah. Well. I wouldn't be surprised if he could," I said.

The judge laughed.

"Miles is an amazing man. With many a talent. But I don't think he can do that," he said.

His belly jiggled with his laughter.

I say that because I could see his waders jiggling around his waist.

Ripples of water flowed out in waves from his wide girth.

"Do you remember that kidnapping?" Miles asked the judge. "The boy with the teddy bear?"

"Why, yes," the judge said. "I do."

"Do you recall the outcome?" I asked the

Stuffed Animal

judge.

The man looked off into the distance.

"Come to think of it? I don't think I do," he said.

"Did the boy die?" Miles asked.

The judge rubbed his nose.

"I don't know. I don't think so," he said. "But I'm not sure. Why do you ask?"

Miles looked at me.

I guess he wanted me to explain.

"Remember the teddy bear?" I asked the judge.

"Yes. Yes, I do," he said. "The mother released pictures. She'd said that if someone saw the bear? Her son would be attached to it."

He looked at Miles and me.

"Why?" he asked slowly.

I looked at Miles.

Miles looked at me.

"Do I want to know?" the judge asked.

Miles made a face at me. He lifted his eyebrows and pointed his head at the judge.

"*You* tell him," Miles said to me.

The judge started to look worried.

"Tell me what?!" he said.

I looked at Miles.

"Tell him," Miles whispered.

I looked at the judge.

He was staring at me. His hands were clutching his fishing pole.

"We found the bear," I said. "At least we *think* we found the bear."

He said nothing.

He just started reeling in his line.

When it was finished, he spoke.

"Okay. That's enough fishing for one day," he said. "Show me that bear."

Chapter 9

Sweat started to bead on the judge's forehead.

"I hate to tell you," he said.

"Hate to tell us what?" Miles asked.

I didn't know if I wanted to know.

I had a feeling I knew what he was going to say.

"I think it's the bear too," the judge said. "Except for the Cajun line that sewed the arm back on? It's exactly the same."

"So what are you going to do?" I asked him.

"*I* can't do anything," he said. "I'm a judge."

I looked at him.

"But *you* can do something about it," he said.

"Me?!" I said. "What can *I* do?!"

The judge looked at Miles.

It was as if he didn't want to tell me what to do.

Like he wasn't *allowed* to.

But Miles could.

"You can contact the parents," Miles said.

He'd said it simply. Like it was no big deal.

"Contact the *parents*?!" I screamed. "Of a kidnapped *kid*?"

Miles and the judge just looked at me.

"What do *I* know about something like that?!" I wailed.

When no one answered? I went on.

"What do I *say* to them?!" I sputtered. "I can't just say 'We found your son's teddy bear.'"

The judge agreed. "No," he said. "You're right. You can't say that without having more details."

That's when I knew I was in deep this time.

"Look, son," Judge Simpkins started. "You've done a great job on the other cases."

Was he kidding?!

This was *nothing* like the other "cases."

Those didn't involve a kidnapping.

Stuffed Animal

Those didn't involve a child. A *missing* child.

"I can't do this," I said aloud.

I didn't care who was listening.

I didn't care what anyone else thought.

I couldn't do this.

I *wouldn't* do this.

This was out of my league.

Totally out of my league.

This was serious. *Truly* serious!

This was for *real*!

"I can't do this," I repeated.

"Yes," the judge said. "Yes you can."

Miles put his arm around my shoulders. "You *can* do this, Dan," he said smoothly. "And you will."

"For the sake of the boy," Judge Simpkins added.

I looked at both of them.

Waited for them to tell me they were joking.

That they would handle this.

But they didn't say those things.

They just stared at me.

Watching me. Closely.

"You can do this, son," Judge Simpkins said.

I shook my head.

"This needs to be handled by a professional," I said.

"If the police get involved? It will become an official investigation," Miles said.

"The media will be all over this again," the judge pointed out.

"Do you want a media circus?" Miles asked me.

I shook my head slowly. "No. But…"

"There are no buts, Dan," Miles said.

"This needs to be done. And you can do it," the judge added.

I felt like I'd been waylaid. Ambushed.

I shook my head.

"I'm not sure about this," I said.

"I'll help you," Miles said.

I looked at the judge.

He shook his head.

"I can't help you, son."

"Why not?" I asked.

I mean, if I were going to do this? I needed as much help as possible.

"I'm sorry. I can't," he repeated.

I looked at him.

I looked at Miles.

"I'll help you, Dan," Miles said. "But the judge can't be involved at all."

I still didn't get why.

"I may be needed in another capacity," Judge Simpkins said. "For a different function."

I still didn't get it.

"Based on what you find out? There might be a need for a judge," he explained.

"And we wouldn't want him to be disqualified for being involved in the investigation," Miles added.

"I wouldn't want to have to recuse myself," the judge said. "Not on something that might be very important."

Chapter 10

My mind was racing.

This was big! Bigger than anything I'd ever done before.

This… mattered.

The other stuff I'd done? The other cases? They didn't really matter.

Sure. They'd mattered to those involved.

But this?

This was big.

Huge!

It was a nationally known case.

At one time? People all over the *country* were looking for this boy.

Heck. I'd been in New York City and my heart

Stuffed Animal

went out to the boy's parents.

And now? This was years later.

Two years, if I'm not mistaken.

How could *I* help?!

"I don't even know where to start," I said aloud.

"You'll figure it out," Judge Simpkins said. "And now? If you don't mind? I'll leave you to your work."

If I didn't mind?

Yes, I minded!

I understood why he couldn't be involved. I did. But I also needed help.

"Do you want me to call my friend?" Judge Simpkins offered.

"Yes," I said. "That would be great."

The guy—that mystery guy—was sure to be able to help.

He always did.

I had no idea who he was. Or what he did. Or who he worked for.

But he always pointed me to the right path.

Elise Leonard

I watched as the judge picked up the phone.

He dialed.

"Hi darlin'," he drawled. "Is the big boss in?"

The judge made a face.

"Oh, that's too bad. Do you know how long he'll be gone?"

I waited to hear the answer.

Judge Simpkins spoke into the phone again.

"It can be that long?" he said.

That didn't sound good.

"Deep cover, you say?" he said into the phone.

That sounded even worse.

"No, no, dear. That's okay. Don't have him ruin a case for me," the judge said.

He listened some more.

"Yes. That's fine. When he gets back, have him give me a ring."

Then the judge hung up the phone.

He rubbed his chin. Or should I say chins.

"Looks like you're on your own on this one, Dan," he said.

I'd figured as much.

Stuffed Animal

"Any idea when he'll get back?" I asked.

The judge shook his head.

"He's deep. Under cover. For him to be deep under cover? It's got to be big," he said.

"Maybe we should wait for him to come back," I said.

The judge scratched his chins.

"No. I don't think so," he replied.

"Why not?" I asked. "He's *much* more qualified than I am."

The judge shook his head.

"If he's deep under cover? We don't know how long he'll be gone."

"But…" I started to argue.

"And there's a good chance he won't come back," the judge said simply. "We can't wait."

A good chance? That he won't come back?!

I still had no idea what the man did. Or for whom he worked.

I knew his job was stressful.

I knew his job was important.

And now I knew that he couldn't help me.

Chapter 11

So. Where to start.

That was the question.

"The bear was found in the yard. Right?" I asked Miles.

"Right," he said.

"But the dogs could have carried it around from anywhere in the yard. Right?"

"Right," Miles agreed.

"So it could have come from any car."

"Right," Miles said for the third time.

Okay. That left us… nowhere.

I was trying to think things out.

Trying to come up with something. Anything.

An idea.

Stuffed Animal

A clue.

Anything!

"How can we narrow this down?" I asked aloud.

"I can't think of a way," Miles replied.

There had been no records of the cars that the old Dan took in.

I kept records. But he hadn't.

So I couldn't even go through records to see which cars came in during the last two or three years.

Just then I heard a dog barking. Loudly.

Viciously.

Then I heard a girlish scream.

I thought of Lucky.

I remembered what the woman had said to me.

I can't put him with a family. It's too risky.

I thought of the little girl outside. The one who had screamed.

She was probably with her parents. Coming to get a part.

I went running to the door. Running to race

outside to help the girl and her family.

Running to save the girl from Lucky.

As I swung open the screen door? I raced outside.

My heart was thumping.

Blood was pumping through my veins.

I could hear it in my ears.

I was trying not to picture the girl getting ripped apart by Lucky.

As I took my second step outside? I was plowed down.

I was hit—head on. Full force.

Hard.

It knocked me back.

Back into the screen door.

I bounced off the screen and sprang back into what had hit me to begin with.

The second crash was as solid as the first.

I was going to feel that tomorrow!

I heard someone shout.

"Call Cujo off me, Dan."

It sounded like Bubba.

Stuffed Animal

"I have to go," I yelled. "I have to save a little girl."

I started running again.

"What little girl?" Bubba screamed after me.

"The one who was being attacked by Lucky," I called over my shoulder.

I kept running.

My head ached from smashing into Bubba's hard head. Twice.

But my head was clearing now. And I couldn't see anyone.

I looked around.

Looked for the little girl.

All I could see was Bubba's car. Well, one of Bubba's cars.

The cherry red Mustang. The classic car he was restoring.

It was glistening out in the sunshine.

The chrome parts blinding me.

By now, Bubba was next to me.

"What little girl?" he asked.

He was out of breath from running.

"The one who screamed," I said.

Lucky came over to us. He was baring his teeth.

Growling.

He was eyeing Bubba.

Bubba pulled out a pocket knife.

He snapped it open.

He waved it at Lucky.

Lucky reacted to the knife.

He hunched down and looked like he would spring.

Right at Bubba.

I looked from Lucky to Bubba.

I looked at the knife.

"Put that thing away," I said to Bubba.

"Not with Cujo on the prowl," he said.

"Put it away," I said.

Bubba didn't move.

Neither did Lucky.

But the dog started to growl.

Low and deep. Menacing.

"Put it away. Now!" I roared.

Chapter 12

"I can't," Bubba said.

Lucky looked like he was going to pounce at any moment.

"Please," I whispered. "Trust me. Put it away. I think he thinks you are trying to hurt him. Or me."

Bubba slowly snapped the knife shut.

He inched the closed knife to his back pocket.

He held out his hands. Palms up. Before him.

I called to Lucky.

"Come here, boy. Come here, Lucky. It's okay. This is Bubba."

I tried to sound calm.

But I wasn't.

Lucky's eyes were hard. Like stone.

No emotion.

"Come on, Lucky. Come here. Bubba is a friend," I said softly.

Bubba kept his eyes on Lucky. But he spoke to me.

"Don't push him if he doesn't want to," Bubba said a little too loudly.

Lucky bared his teeth and growled again.

"He thinks you are yelling at me," I told Bubba. "We need to show him that you are a friend."

As usual, Bubba was Bubba.

"What do you want me to do? Smell your butt?!" he asked me.

I was nervous.

Nervous about seeing my friend mutilated.

Nervous about Lucky being put down before he got a chance to see how good life could be.

But mostly? Nervous about seeing my friend mangled.

So I laughed. A nervous laugh, but a laugh.

And the moment I laughed? Lucky stopped growling.

Stuffed Animal

I called Lucky again.

He inched over.

Bubba stood still. His hands were out. His palms up.

He looked like a statue.

A trembling statue, but a statue.

Lucky smelled Bubba's hands. He drew his snout back quickly.

"Must be the smell of gasoline," Bubba said softly.

I didn't know if he was talking to me or Lucky.

"I'm not going to hurt you, Lucky," he said softly.

Lucky inched closer to Bubba.

Bubba didn't move.

"I'm here to see a friend," Bubba all but whispered.

Lucky sniffed Bubba.

"I'm scared, boss," he whispered.

I tried not to smile.

"If that dog bites me? Where he's sniffing? There'll be no little Bubbas running around.

Ever!"

I had to laugh.

"Lucky might do the world a favor," I replied.

The dog moved from Bubba's front to his back.

He was still sniffing like crazy.

Finally, he stopped and stepped back.

He came back to Bubba's front side. Then he stuck his head under Bubba's extended hand.

Bubba turned his hand and started petting Lucky.

"You're not such a bad dog," Bubba told Lucky.

The situation was under control.

"I have to go," I said.

"Where?' Bubba asked.

I looked around. "To find that little girl."

"Little girl?" Bubba asked me.

"The one who screamed before."

Bubba's face turned red. Beet red.

Chapter 13

"That was me," Bubba said quietly. "I thought Lucky was going to attack. You know. Rip my neck out."

That made me laugh.

"You scream just like a little girl," I said.

Bubba tried to look insulted.

He failed.

His shoulders slumped.

"Yeah, well. If you'd been in my shoes? You might have done the same thing."

I smirked.

"I might have screamed. But not like a little girl."

"Okay. Okay. Can we let it drop?" Bubba

asked.

I smiled again.

"So where'd you get Cujo? I mean Lucky," he asked.

"The animal shelter brought him here. He's been terribly abused."

We were walking as we talked. Lucky was beside us. Limping.

Bubba watched Lucky and nodded.

"Yeah. I can see it now," he said.

We walked some more.

"Where are we going?" he asked.

"I don't know about *you*," I said with a grin. "But I'm looking around."

"For what?" Bubba asked.

"For cars that might have come in during the past two or three years."

"I might be able to help you with that," Bubba said.

"Really? How?" I asked.

"Dan—I mean the old Dan—was getting old. He needed help around here. So I helped him out."

Stuffed Animal

I nodded.

"You know which cars came in lately?" I asked.

He shrugged. "Most of them."

"Can you point them out?" I asked.

We walked through the whole yard.

I made a list of vehicles and their VIN numbers.

"This should be a start," I told Bubba.

"A start for what?" he asked.

"To find out how that stuffed animal came in here."

"Oh. Right. The kidnapped kid," he said.

By then we were back at the office.

Miles was in my small living room. Watching TV and eating a bag of microwave popcorn.

"Want some?" he offered.

"Yeah," Bubba said.

He plopped down on the sofa next to Miles.

"What's on?" Bubba asked.

"Not much. Just flipping through channels," Miles replied.

"Want some popcorn?" Miles called to me.

I was in my office. Firing up the computer.

"No thanks," I said.

"What are you doing?" Miles asked.

"I'm going to run down the list," I answered.

He came to the doorway.

"What list?" he asked.

"The list of possible cars Bubba and I made up."

"You've got a *list*?" he asked.

"Yup. Bubba helped Dan these last few years. So he knew the cars that came in recently. Within the last three years or so."

Miles looked excited.

"That perfect. Let's get to work," he said.

We started tracking down the owners of all the cars on the list.

If the owner only owned the car for a year or two? We went to the previous owner, and wrote that down as well.

Bubba came into the office.

"There's nothing on TV," he said.

Stuffed Animal

"We could use your help with this list of owners," I said.

Bubba came to my desk.

He looked over my shoulder.

He pulled a face. "That's one long list," he said.

"Yes," I agreed. "But I think it's doable. *If* we have three people working on it," I added.

"Want to help us?" Miles asked Bubba.

Bubba shrugged.

"Yeah. I guess. I'm not doing much of anything else at the moment."

"So what now, boss?" Miles asked me.

Chapter 14

"Would you guys *please* stop calling me boss?!" I snapped.

Miles smiled and looked at Bubba.

Bubba grinned.

Then he mumbled to Miles. "It's just too easy!"

I rolled my eyes.

"Okay. Let's take every third name on the list and call that one," I said.

"What?!" Bubba asked.

"I'll take the first name. Miles? You take the second. And Bubba will take the third. Then I'll take the fourth. Miles, the fifth. And Bubba? You'll take the sixth."

Miles nodded. But Bubba looked confused.

Stuffed Animal

"Why do you always have to make everything so *complicated*?!" Bubba asked me.

Bubba grabbed the list out of my hand.

He took the first page.

He tore it in three pieces. Sideways.

He handed me a strip.

"You call these people," he said to me.

He handed Miles a strip.

"You call these folks," Bubba told Miles.

He waved the last strip.

"And I'll call these people," he said.

He pointed to the rest of the list.

"When we're done with these? We'll do the same with the names on those pages," he said.

Hm. I couldn't believe it.

Bubba had a plan.

And it seemed to make sense.

"Okay," I said. "Sounds like a plan."

"But what do we *say* to these people?" Miles asked as he waved his strip of list.

He had a point.

I hadn't thought of that part yet.

This was obviously a plan in progress.

"We need to ask them about the kidnapping. If they were involved," I said.

Bubba shook his head. "That's not going to work. If they were involved? They're going to lie about it!"

"I think that over the phone? I can't tell if people are lying," Miles said.

"Yeah. I need to see their faces, too," Bubba said.

They were right.

We'd need to go to their homes. See their faces while we asked them questions.

See how they'd respond.

"Okay. Well, that changes everything," I said.

I looked at the strips of paper in our hands.

"Miles? You can come with me. I'm not a great judge of character."

That made Bubba laugh.

"Yeah, Dan," he said. "You were on Wall Street so long? People could lie right to your face. And you'd never know the difference!"

Stuffed Animal

I would have argued.

I *did* have my pride.

But he was right.

I mean, look at my wife.

Patti? She must have been lying to me. But I had no clue.

"We now have two teams and three lists," I said.

I made a face at Bubba.

He'd ripped up my list into three parts. And now we only needed two.

Bubba rolled his eyes.

"Has anyone ever told you that you're anal?!" he said with a heavy sigh.

He snatched the list from my hand. And before I could stop him? He tore that one in two.

He handed a smaller strip to Miles.

"There," Bubba said.

He waggled the first, larger strip and the little skinnier list.

"We each have half now," he said.

I looked at Miles.

He was standing there with two strips of paper. A fatter one and a skinnier one.

"Can you live with *that*?!" Bubba asked me.

I couldn't help myself.

The words just slipped out.

"My poor list," I said. "It's a big mess now."

"Anal, Dan," Bubba said. "You're too anal!"

"Look. Let's just work on a list of questions to ask the car owners," Miles said.

"I think we should just ask them: *Did you kidnap that kid?* And see how they react," Bubba said.

Chapter 15

"You can't just come out and say it like that," I argued.

"Why not?" Bubba asked.

I looked at Miles.

He shrugged.

"You know? Why can't we? We're not the police," Miles said slowly.

"You don't think there's a better approach?" I asked Miles.

"Not one that will get results as quickly," he answered.

"Ha!" Bubba said. "So I was *right*?"

It was a rare occurrence.

Even Bubba looked surprised.

"You know what? I think you might be," Miles said.

"Okay, then. If no one can come up with anything better? I guess we should go with that then," I said.

What did *we* know?!

We weren't cops.

We weren't PIs.

We weren't interrogators.

"Okay," Miles said.

"Okay," Bubba said.

Then Bubba giggled. "I can't believe we're going to use my method. Cool!"

"We'll start with this first page and see where we get. Call us on my cell if you get any bites," I told Bubba.

Bubba looked at his list and planned his best route.

Miles and I did the same thing.

"Do you want to rewrite the list so we put the people together by location?" I asked Miles and Bubba.

Stuffed Animal

"Anal, Dan," Bubba said loudly.

"But with gas so expensive, maybe we should," Miles put in.

I looked at Bubba.

I tried not to give him my "See? I told you so!" look, but I don't think I succeeded.

"Well, okay. Yeah. Maybe," Bubba said slowly.

We put all the scraps together and had to reassign the list.

"That's only the first page," I said. "I think we need to do this with all three pages."

I looked to Miles so he could back me up.

Miles looked at Bubba.

"It does make sense," Miles told Bubba.

"Anal," was all Bubba said.

"*Practical*," was my response.

We got out a couple of county maps. Then we taped them up on the wall.

Then I went to my desk. To get some post-it notes. So we could mark off the locations.

When I turned around? Bubba had already

stuck a bunch of pushpins into the maps. (And the wall.)

"You're putting holes in the wall," I snapped at Bubba.

"Anal," Bubba said. "Anal, Dan."

Well, the damage was already done.

I cringed with each additional pin he stuck in the wall.

But it did make it easier to see where we had to go.

I chose the people on the west half of the maps. And Bubba would take the east.

And once this was done? I planned to spackle and repaint the wall.

Actually all the walls were a bit shabby.

I guess I could repaint the entire office.

I know. I know.

Anal.

Chapter 16

I called Bubba. "How many people have you gotten through?" I asked him.

"I'm halfway done. How about you guys?"

"We've been through about ten," I told Bubba. "But so far? No one seems suspicious. They all remember the kidnapping. But none seem to have any connection."

"Same here," Bubba said.

"One couple seemed a bit weird. But I think they were just weird people. Nothing to do with the kidnapping. Just everyday sort of weird."

Bubba laughed. "Yeah, I've had my share of those, too."

"Okay," I said. "Keep in touch. We're at

another place now and have to go in."

"Okay," Bubba said. "I'll call you if I need you for anything."

We walked toward the front door.

"So how is *he* faring?" Miles asked me.

I shrugged. "Same as we are. No one is sticking out. Some weird people. But no one is really popping out at him."

We were at the front door.

I rang the doorbell.

A man came to the door.

He wasn't old. But he wasn't that young either.

"Can I help ya'll?" he asked.

"We have a few questions to ask you," Miles said.

"A car of yours is in my junkyard," I added.

He opened his door.

I knew instantly that the man was not married.

How did I know?

By the décor.

When we walked through the door? A bass fish on a plaque popped out at us and started singing.

Stuffed Animal

It looked like a fisherman's trophy. But it wasn't.

The bass was lip syncing to the song *Take Me to the River*.

Miles was staring up at the fish plaque.

"That's the strangest thing I've ever seen!" he said.

The man laughed. "You've never seen a Boogie Bass before?"

Miles shook his head. "Nope."

I'd seen them on TV, but never knew anyone who'd owned one.

I thought it was funny when I'd seen it. But there was no way—NO WAY!—Patti would have ever let something like that in her house.

There was another Boogie Bass on the far side of the man's house.

He pointed to it.

"That one sings *I Will Survive*," the man said. "I think they're a real hoot!"

Miles was looking back and forth between the two.

Miles was speechless at first.

"Yes," Miles said. "They certainly are something else."

We followed the man to the other side of the room. He pressed a button on the plaque. And the fish popped out at us and started singing.

The man was correct. It was singing *I Will Survive.*

The man had fish lamps. Fish telephones. Fish posters on his walls.

His couch was covered in fish fabric.

He had fish pillows on his fish-covered couch and chairs.

His curtains? Fish scenes.

He had stuffed fish, plastic fish, metal fish, and any other kind of fish decoration you could imagine.

This guy was into fishing.

He had a fishing pole strewn across his couch.

There was a pile of red fishing line sitting in a big pile on the carpet.

Even the *carpet* had a fish pattern.

Stuffed Animal

"Sorry about the mess," the man said. "I'm in the middle of re-spooling my reel."

"No problem," I said.

He picked up his rod and went back to work.

"So. What can I help ya'll with?" he asked.

The reel whirred as he worked.

"We want to know if you know anything about that kidnapping," Miles said.

"The one that happened a couple of years ago," I added.

The whirring stopped. Briefly. Then it started up again.

"No. No. No. No. Can't say that I do," he said.

His smile was forced.

"No, no, no," he repeated. "Don't know nothing about that."

I looked at Miles.

He looked at me.

Then Miles spoke. "That's a double negative. If you 'don't know nothing' then, what you're *really* saying, is that you *do* know *something*."

The guy went stark white.

"Look. Who *are* you guys? The police? Private dicks? From the insurance place?"

Miles looked at me.

I looked back at Miles.

We'd hit a nerve.

I knew Miles was only trying to correct the man's grammar.

But somehow? We'd hit on something.

"Look. I swear. I had nothing to do with it. You have to ask Earl."

I looked at Miles.

He looked at me.

I took out a pad and pen.

"Earl?" I asked.

"Yeah. Earl. The boy's daddy."

Now it was my turn to go pale.

"The boy's *father*?!" I asked.

The man's leg started twitching. He was nervous.

Mighty nervous.

"Just go ask Earl. I had nothin' to do with it. All I got was two hundred dollars. That's all."

Chapter 17

I was confused.

"Are we talking about the same thing?" I asked the man.

"The kidnapping? Two years ago? Of the little boy?" Miles asked.

The man looked at Miles. "Yeah. That's the one. But I had nothin' to do with it. It was all Earl."

"You'd better give us Earl's address," Miles said to the nervous man.

That's when it hit me.

I knew something seemed off to me. But the fish stuff everywhere threw me off my game.

It was the fishing line on the floor.

It wasn't the normal blue or aqua or green.

It was red.

I pointed to the pile of fishing line.

"What's that stuff called?" I asked the man.

"Cajun line," he said.

I looked at Miles. "That's what was used to sew the arm back on the teddy bear."

The man's other leg started jumping.

He was jumping and twitching so badly? I thought he'd shake himself apart.

Miles stared at the man.

"Did you or did you not sew the arm back on the boy's teddy bear with that Cajun line?"

The man blanched.

"We'll take that as a yes," I said.

I was furious!

I was also a little scared.

We'd caught the kidnapper. But there were no police around.

No way to lock him up.

I took out my phone.

"I'm calling the police," I said.

Stuffed Animal

"Look. Please. Earl said we'd never get caught. No one got hurt. Please."

That struck me as odd.

"What do you mean, no one got hurt?" I asked.

"The boy. He's fine. He's back home with Earl and Frannie," the man said quickly.

"He's alive?" Miles asked the man.

"Yeah, yeah. He's alive. Look. I'll take you there. Just don't call the police."

I looked at Miles.

He looked at me.

Miles shrugged.

"I never *did* hear the results of the kidnapping. Maybe the boy *is* still alive," Miles said.

"He is! He is! I'll prove it to you!"

The man was begging.

"Please. Please! Let me prove it to you. No one got hurt!"

Miles and I spoke together briefly.

We decided that we didn't know if we should go to the police yet. But if we let the man prove himself, we might find out the real story.

We could always bring in the police later.

He was a small, slight man. If he were unarmed? He couldn't hurt us.

Miles and I, though, could make short work out of him.

"Strip to your underwear," I told him.

The man started stripping right away.

No questions asked.

Miles threw me a look. He was confused.

"He can't have a weapon on him if he's in his underwear," I told Miles.

Miles smiled.

The man stood in his boxers and undershirt.

Need I mention? The boxers were covered in fish. And the t-shirt? A silly cartoon fish was drawn on the front.

Not only was this guy not married? I doubted he'd *ever* find a woman. Not with *his* taste.

"Now let's go to Earl's house," Miles said.

Chapter 18

On the way, I called Bubba.

"Quit the search," I said. "I think we got it."

"Okay," he said. "I'll wait for you at the yard."

"All right," I said. "But we may be a while."

Just then, we showed up to a gorgeous house. Almost a mansion.

It just kept going and going and going.

It sprawled from the center. The center part was grand. It had four pillars with three arches. The windows were sky high. Cathedral ceilings.

There were at least four more sections of the house as it kept on spreading across the estate.

One section was an elegant sunroom. It was built with tinted glass. Floor to ceiling tinted glass. So one could see out, but not in.

The place was magnificent.

There was no other word for it.

"Your friend Earl lives here?" I asked.

"Impressive. Huh?" the man asked.

"Yes," I said. "You could say that."

"His mortgage payment must be a monster," Miles said softly.

He was looking at the entire house. From left to right, then back again.

His head was moving like he was looking at a tennis match.

That's how large the house was.

"Earl married up," the man said with a snort.

We got out of the car and took the man to the front door.

We had to walk around a Cadillac Escalade.

There was another car in the driveway, but parked to the side.

"I brought the stuffed animal," Miles said.

I rang the bell.

It took a while. But a woman came to the door. A child stood behind her. Hiding behind her legs.

Stuffed Animal

"Is Earl home?" I asked.

"Yes," she said. Then she called for Earl.

Earl came to the door. He took one look at the little man and started heading out the door.

He tried to close it behind him.

"Who are these people, Earl?" the wife asked.

"None of your business," Earl said nastily.

I didn't like his tone.

I think I summed up this situation in an instant.

I pushed open the door.

"We will have this conversation inside," I said. "All together," I added.

Earl tried to bully his way outside.

Miles and I stood in his way. Let's just say we "directed" him back inside.

When the little boy saw the teddy bear, he screeched with glee. "Bear-Bear!"

The mother turned with surprise to her son. Then she looked at us.

"How did you get Bear-Bear?" she asked us.

She looked suspicious and her eyes narrowed.

"We *all* need to talk," I said.

"I had nothing to do with it," the little man said. "It was all *your* idea, Earl."

"Shut up, you idiot!" Earl snapped.

The woman looked confused. "Sweetheart," she said to her son. "Why don't you go in the kitchen and play with Bear-Bear?"

She was a good mother. Protecting her son.

She didn't even know what was going on. But she was protecting her son. Putting him out of harms way.

She went to an intercom. "Mom? Dad? I'm sending the baby in to the kitchen. Can you please watch him for me for a few minutes?"

"What's wrong?" an elderly woman demanded.

"Frannie," Earl pleaded. "Don't listen to these men. *Any* of them."

He threw a look at his friend. A dirty look.

Frannie took her hand off the intercom button.

"I think someone has some explaining to do," I said with anger.

I was looking at Earl.

"Who do you think you are?!" he demanded.

Stuffed Animal

"Coming in to *my* house?! Get out of my house!"

Frannie looked at me. "It is my house too, sir. Please stay and explain yourself."

I nodded. "I don't know much," I started. "I do know that your son was kidnapped about two years ago."

"Yes," she said. "But we paid the ransom and he was returned. Unharmed."

I looked at the nervous little man. Then I looked at Earl.

I now had all of my answers.

"I own a junkyard and found, ah, Bear-Bear. I then found this guy. He brought us here."

"You *idiot*!" Earl spit out to his friend.

"In the last few years. Have you been having financial difficulties?" I asked Frannie.

"No," she said. "Not that I know of."

"There. You've got your answer. Now get out!"

"Earl," Frannie said. "Why are you being so rude?"

"He's always rude," an older woman said from the doorway.

Chapter 19

An older man stood beside her. He was holding the little boy. The boy was holding Bear-Bear.

I turned to Earl's friend. "Tell them what you told us."

He looked at Earl. But then he looked at Frannie, Miles, the older couple and me.

"It was all Earl," he said. "He made me do it."

"For two hundred dollars," I added.

Earl's head snapped toward his friend. "You are *such* an idiot!"

Everyone looked at the boy. Then at Bear-Bear.

They too put two and two together.

The older man took out his cell phone. "I'm calling the police."

"Good," Earl said. "These people need to be arrested for trespassing."

Stuffed Animal

No one said a word. No one argued with Earl. We let Earl think that he was in control. Until the police came.

Then the story came out.

It was just as I'd suspected.

"The balloon payments. The mortgage. I was about to lose my house!" Earl shouted.

"So you had our son *kidnapped*?! You made your *son* go through that? You made *me* go through that? So you could extort money from my parents?!"

"Hey," Earl said. "They've got plenty! It wasn't a big deal for them!"

Frannie gasped.

She looked at her parents. "You were right all along. He was only after my money."

"And you were an idiot for asking them to stop giving you money!" Earl spat out at his wife.

"I wanted to show them that you *loved* me. That you didn't care about the money. I wanted to prove to them that you could make it on your own. That *we* could make it on our own! I *told* you that we couldn't afford this house. I didn't even *want* this house! It's way too big for our little family."

"*I* wanted the house. I put up with you and your stinking parents to *get* it. I *deserved* this house."

"So you had our son *kidnapped*?"

Earl grinned. "Hey. I paid off the mortgage, didn't I? And I had extra to buy the Escalade!"

His laugh was sinister.

"You're under arrest," a policeman said as he handcuffed Earl.

"You're all idiots," Earl spat out as the officer dragged Earl from the room.

What a mess. I felt so badly for Frannie.

"I'm so sorry," I said to her softly.

She shook her head. "Please. Don't be. You did me a favor. I finally saw his true colors. I should thank you for that."

Frannie's parents ran to her side.

"We tried to stay away because it was hard to hold our tongues about Earl," her mother said.

"But now you know the truth," her father said.

Frannie looked at her parents. "Well, it was

Stuffed Animal

your money that actually paid off the mortgage on this house. So, really, *you* own it. Want to move in to help me raise your grandson?"

Their eyes were filled with tears.

"We'd love nothing more," they said in unison.

I watched as they embraced and cried together.

They'd been through a lot in these last few minutes.

A wife lost her husband. A son lost his father.

A marriage was destroyed.

A woman's core belief of her union was ruined.

But, on the other hand, a couple gained their daughter and grandson.

My wish for them? That they heal.

They have each other, so they will. In time.

My thoughts went to Lucky.

Of healing. Of time.

My thoughts went to Patti.

Of healing. Of time.

My thoughts went to Rosa.

Of healing. Of time.

Then my phone rang.

I saw it was my office number. It was Bubba.

"Hey," I said. "We're on our way back soon."

"How'd it go?" Bubba asked.

"We caught the kidnapper and his sidekick."

"The boy okay?" Bubba asked.

"Perfect. He was glad to get his bear back."

Bubba chuckled. "Good."

"How's Lucky?" I asked.

"He didn't rip my head off when I got here."

That made me laugh. "That's good," I said.

"Yeah, well, we have another problem."

"Another problem?" I asked. "What?"

"One of the cats found a vial of poison in one of the cars."

"What?" I asked.

"I found a dead cat in one of the cars. On the front seat. Passenger side. She must have been playing with the vial. I found her dead. There's a hole in the cap. A tooth must have punctured it. The poor cat's dead. It has to be poison."

"Okay," I said with a heavy sigh. "I'll be home soon to take care of everything. Keep that bottle!"

Chapter 20

I got back to the junkyard.

Bubba was there, waiting.

"So what happened?" he asked.

I sighed heavily.

"You wouldn't believe it if I told you," I said.

Bubba smiled. "Try me."

I snorted a laugh.

"We met this fish guy. A real prize, if you know what I mean."

Bubba nodded.

"He makes a comment. Then Miles corrects his grammar," I went on.

Bubba laughed. "That sounds like Miles."

"Right," I smiled. "And before we know it? The guy's confessing to the kidnapping!"

Bubba cracked up. "You're kidding!"

"No. Then he takes us to the house of the kidnapped boy," I said.

"And?"

"And it turned out that the creepy father *arranged* the kidnapping!"

"No way!"

"Yes! And the wife? I felt really sorry for her. She knew nothing about it!"

Bubba shook his head.

"Some people don't deserve to have kids," he said softly.

I looked at Bubba.

"You want to have children?" I asked him.

He smiled at the thought. "Some day."

I thought of him as a father.

"You know, Bubba? You'd make a good dad," I said. And I meant it.

He smiled. "Thanks. You would too, Dan."

I don't know why. But his comment pleased me.

"I've always wanted kids. But Patti didn't want to ruin her figure."

Stuffed Animal

Bubba made a face.

"What did you see in that woman?" he asked me.

I shrugged. "I was blinded by love, I guess."

He nodded. "I guess."

We stood there. Each with our own thoughts.

Finally, I broke the silence.

"I should bury that cat now," I said softly.

Bubba nodded.

This was hard for me to do.

My mind went to Rosa. How she'd just buried her father. A *good* father. A good man.

I knew that burying the cat wasn't like burying one's father. But it was still a loss. I was still saddened.

"Want me to help?" Bubba asked quietly.

"No," I said. "I can do it alone."

Bubba nodded.

I went to the shed. To get the shovel.

I walked to the cat. It took a while to get there.

Lucky and a few other dogs walked with me.

My mind was racing.

I needed to track down that vial of poison.

Where did it come from?

What was it used for?

I thought of the poor cat. I thought of Lucky. I thought of Earl and Frannie and their son.

Lucky was limping along. His body still oozing with his wounds.

"Animals are happy to survive," I said aloud.

No one was there to hear. But I didn't care.

I looked at Lucky again.

"They're happy if they can get their basic needs met," I added.

I thought about that.

I thought about human greed.

Human wants.

Human excess.

I thought about Earl.

Then I heard Lucky bark.

He had a ball in his mouth and his tail was wagging.

Humans can learn a lot from animals.

Now that Dan has solved *this* problem, please read the next **JUNKYARD DAN** book, entitled **POISON, ANYONE?**, to find out about the poison found in one of the cars. Is it really poison? And if so, was it used to kill someone? Was it used in a homicide? Was it used in a suicide? Was it used for science? Find out by reading the *next* book in the series!

And we have a few **other** series that you might like too:

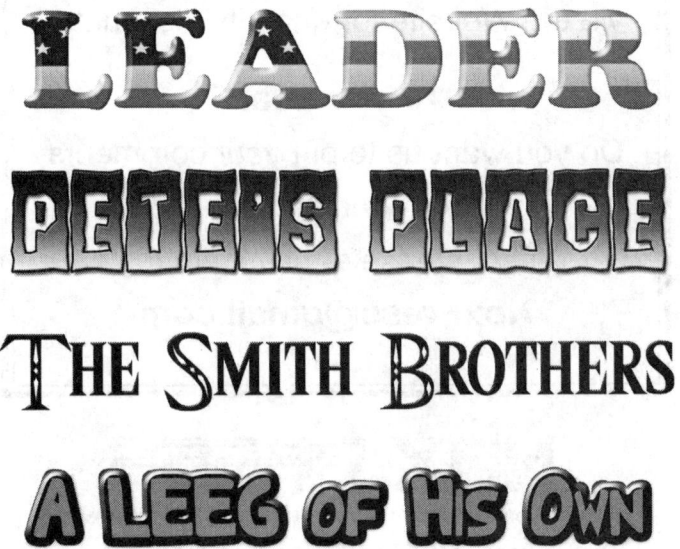

LEADER

PETE'S PLACE

THE SMITH BROTHERS

A LEEG OF HIS OWN

Want to read more NOX PRESS books?

Go online to
www.NoxPress.com
to see what's being released!

Books can easily be purchased online
or you can contact **Nox Press**
via the Website for quantity discounts.

Are you a fan?

Do you want us to put *your* comments
up on our Website?
If so, please e-mail them to:
NoxPress@gmail.com

NOX PRESS
books for that extra kick to give you more power
www.NoxPress.com